THE·LAST STRAW

Fredrick H. Thury

Illustrated by Vlasta van Kampen

Dedicated to Alexis and Sara.
F.H.T.

For my daughter Saskia. This camel is for you.
V.v.K.

Text Copyright © 1998 by Fredrick H. Thury
Illustrations Copyright © 1998 by Vlasta Van Kampen

First published in Canada in 1998 by Key Porter Books Limited
70 The Esplanade, Toronto, Ontario, Canada M5E 1R2

This edition first published in 2005 by Zero To Ten
Ltd, a division of the Evans Publishing Group,
2A Portman Mansions,
Chiltern St.
London W1U 6NR

A CIP catalogue record for this book is available from the British Library.

ISBN 1-84089-389-3

Printed and bound in Hong Kong

Hoshmakaka, the old camel, was asleep in the desert night. He dreamed of all the water in the world and a hump that would hold an entire sea.

Hearing voices, Hoshmakaka opened one eye. "Hoshmakaka. Hoshmakaka."

Reluctantly, Hoshmakaka opened the other eye. "Why should I wake up?" he grumbled.

The sand whirled up into the moonlit sky. "You have been chosen," the voices whispered.

The sand seemed to shift again. "You will carry gifts to a baby king."

"Who are you?" Hoshmakaka wanted to know, for he was an old camel and felt he had earned his sleep.

"You will carry frankincense, myrrh, and gold. The wise men have chosen you."

Hoshmakaka got up very slowly. "Why me? If these men are so wise, don't they know about my joints? My gout? My sciatica? What did you say I am to carry? How much will it weigh?

"Besides, I have other commitments. There's a water-drinking competition in Rangal. Then I really must go to the cud-chewing convention in Beemish."

The sand blew furiously, cutting into the black night. Hoshmakaka was startled and decided he had better do as the voices said. Who knew what made the sand move like creatures with great wings?

"When do I start?" he asked carefully.

"Today." With that, the sand voices disappeared, and it was morning.

It was still early as the servants of the wise men placed the precious gifts onto Hoshmakaka's back. The young camels ran to their good friend. They all looked up to him because he was old, and they thought him wise.

"You must be a very special camel," they sighed.

"I am very special." Hoshmakaka puffed out his chest in pride and then said something a little foolish. "I'm not so old. I'm still as strong as ten horses. And I have been chosen to carry rich gifts to the new baby king."

"Can we come too?" asked the youngest camel, who never wanted to be left behind. "Aren't we your friends?" shouted another.

"You can walk beside me," Hoshmakaka replied in his most regal voice. And the long journey began.

At noon, a herd of mountain goats came into view. Hoshmakaka thought that they had come a long way from their mountain home in the north.

"What is it you want?" Hoshmakaka called out.

"We have heard tell of the new king who is to be born. Please, take our humble gift with you. It's milk for the king."

"You want me to carry milk?" Hoshmakaka sputtered in shock. "I am not a milk-bearing camel. I am not ordinary, like you."

The young camels chorused, "No, he is not ordinary." They looked up to him with their big brown eyes. "He's strong. Why, he's as strong as ten horses."

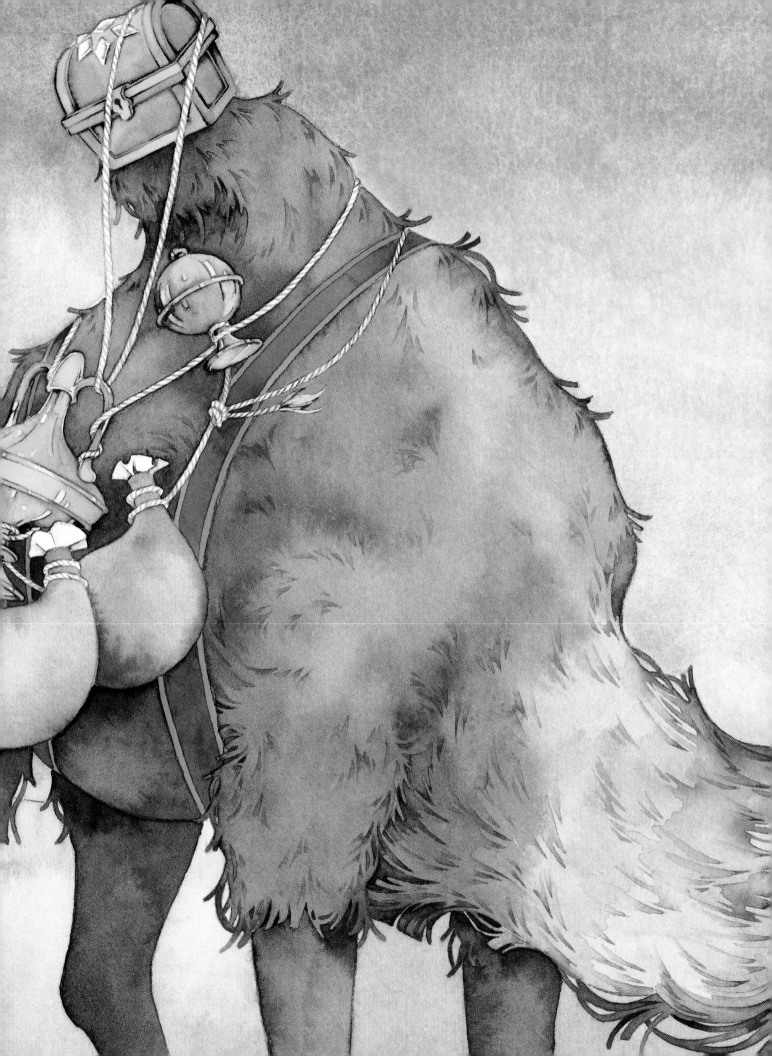

Hoshmakaka muttered to himself,
"My joints. My gout. My sciatica." Aloud
he said grandly, "Give me your gift."

At one o'clock he was stopped by a family of millers.

"Look!" said the youngest camel, "They're carrying bags of ground corn. Do you suppose they're for the new king?"

"They will have to carry it themselves," Hoshmakaka replied. "They can follow that star like the rest of us."

The young camels crowded around Hoshmakaka eagerly. "But you're so strong. You're as strong as ten horses."

Hoshmakaka felt weary just looking at the bags. But he said to the millers, "Give me your heavy bags. I'll carry them."

At two o'clock the next day young ladies gave Hoshmakaka
their fine silks. "At least the cloth doesn't weigh anything," he thought.

At three o'clock an old man in fine clothes gave him two rare birds in silver cages.

At four o'clock some merchants gave him
pillars of oak that came all the way from Lebanon.

At five o'clock a group of bakers gave him their finest sweetmeats and pastries.

At six o'clock the sun finally went down, and the crowds melted into the coming night.

Hoshmakaka gratefully sank into the sand. In the kind darkness he didn't have to pretend he was as strong as ten horses.

Hoshmakaka became aware that it didn't seem as dark as usual. He looked up and saw the splendour of the skies and the special brightness of the star he had been following. He fell asleep wondering about the sand voices and the wings he had thought he could almost see.

But as the sun rose over the desert hills, it was hard to remember the wonder of that star. For the new day brought new pains and new burdens for Hoshmakaka.

"I don't think I will make it. I can't carry any more. My legs are getting weaker. My gout. My sciatica. My joints. I'm too loaded down."

Word of the caravan had spread like sand before a desert wind. People lined the route holding up their gifts for Hoshmakaka to take to the baby king. There were jars full of honey and baskets of money. There were jewels and beads and large rolls of leather. And last but not least there were twenty gallons of wine.

Hoshmakaka moaned to himself, "This will bring me to ruin, this fruit of the vine."

But then the youngest camel cried out, "Look! There! It's Bethlehem. You've made it, Hoshmakaka. You are as strong as ten horses."

Hoshmakaka knew he could just do it if he did not stop until he arrived at the spot beneath the star. He could. He knew he could.

Just then, out of the growing darkness, a small voice said, "I have a gift
for the baby."

Hoshmakaka looked down on a tiny child. "Please, child, no more gifts."

"It has no weight. It's long and light. It's for the king who is born this night. It's little," the child added.

"Too little is too much," Hoshmakaka whispered.

"Didn't I hear them say you were as strong as ten horses?" asked the child.

"Well, yes, I am – sort of. But my joints. My gout." Hoshmakaka looked into the child's eyes, and his heart melted. "Yes, child. Give it to me, this smaller-than-small gift. What harm can it do?"

"It's for his bed. It's all I have."

"No problem at all," said Hoshmakaka bravely, if foolishly.

All this time Hoshmakaka had kept walking because he knew if he stopped, he could not start again. Now he could see that the star shone down upon a lowly stable.

"Child, do it now. Place your straw upon my back as I approach the new king."

Hoshmakaka entered the stable. "My knees are loosening. My legs, they wobble. My back is breaking. Will this last straw cause me to fall?"

And with that, Hoshmakaka fell to his knees. "Oh my," he thought, "this is no way for a camel to behave. They will say that Hoshmakaka the weak camel, Hoshmakaka the proud camel, should not have travelled this far."

The wise men noticed Hoshmakaka. Quickly they, too, knelt.
"They're mocking me now. Falling on their knees, heads bent over like
gnarled old trees."

Then, from the humble manger, a tiny hand reached out and touched Hoshmakaka. His pain seemed to disappear. He could no longer feel his burden.

Hoshmakaka whispered to the baby, "Hosanna from Hoshmakaka. Accept these gifts kindly. They come from far and wide, brought by a beast who once acted blindly."

From that time on there was no burden, great or small, that Hoshmakaka would not gladly carry.